Winter Visitors

Winter Visitors

by Elizabeth Lee O'Donnell

illustrated by Carol Schwartz

Morrow Junior Books
New York

Watercolors were used for the full-color illustrations.
The text type is 16-point Epitome Medium.

Text copyright © 1997 by Elizabeth Lee O'Donnell
Illustrations copyright © 1997 by Carol Schwartz

Printed in Singapore at Tien Wah Press.

1 2 3 4 5 6 7 8 9 10

Library of Congress Cataloging-in-Publication Data
O'Donnell, Elizabeth Lee.
Winter visitors/by Elizabeth Lee O'Donnell; illustrated by Carol Schwartz.
p. cm.
Summary: After a snowfall a variety of animals take shelter in a house.
ISBN 0-688-13063-1 (trade)—ISBN 0-688-13064-X (library)
[1. Winter—Fiction.   2. Animals—Fiction.   3. Stories in rhyme.   4. Counting.]
I. Schwartz, Carol, ill.   II. Title.   PZ8.3.O2875Wi 1997   [E]—dc20   96-38689   CIP AC

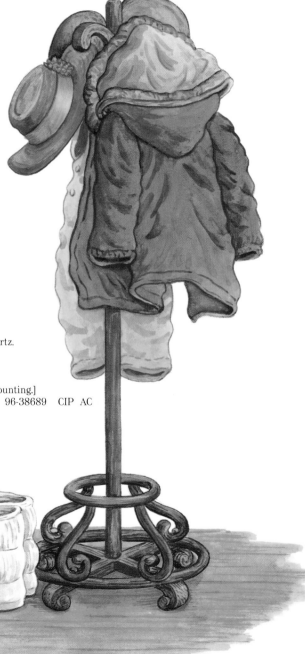

For Mary and my Sophie
—E.L.O'D.

For Zak
—C.S.

After snowfall, outside calls.
"Let's walk in the woods," I say.
"Mer-ow," says Sophie O'Shay.

Outside is crisp and cold, all blue and white.
Silent. Quiet. No one in sight.

The white birch rattles; snow sifts down.
Sophie shakes each paw and frowns.

"Let's go home," I say.

"Mer-ow," says Sophie O'Shay.

Ten wild turkeys are gobbling through our door!

Nine feisty chickadees
splutter from the floor.

Eight hungry snow hares pick the biggest mums.
"Hey," I say. "Go away. Those are Mom's!"

Seven pesky red squirrels
climb the blue hat stand.

Six rollicking fox cubs play at catch-me-if-you-can.

Five eager beavers fell the rocking chair.
"Hey," I say. "That's my dad's. Don't you dare!"

Four greedy blue jays bicker in the kitchen.

Three wide-eyed deer crunch autumn's best pippins.

Two roly-poly raccoons fish for hidden sweets.
"Hey," I say. "Stay away from my treats!"

One two-striped skunk heads for Sophie's plate.

And...

two raccoons drop their loot,
three deer follow suit,
four jays spread their wings,
five beavers stop midswing,
six cubs prick their ears,
seven squirrels peer through gear,

eight hares spit out stems,
nine chickadees go still as gems,
ten turkeys fluff their feathers.
And I ... sigh.

Outside is crisp and cold, all blue and white.
Rackety. Clackety. All but one in sight.

"Mer-ow," says Sophie O'Shay.